Presents
FOR
Santa

by Harriet Ziefert
illustrated by Laura Rader

PUFFIN

Puffin Books
Published by the Penguin Group
Penguin Putnam Books for Young Readers, 345 Hudson Street,
New York, New York 10014, U.S.A.
Penguin Books Ltd, 27 Wrights Lane, London W8 5TZ, England
Penguin Books Australia Ltd, Ringwood, Victoria, Australia
Penguin Books Canada Ltd, 10 Alcorn Avenue, Toronto, Ontario, Canada M4V 3B2
Penguin Books (N.Z.) Ltd, 182-190 Wairau Road, Auckland 10, New Zealand
Penguin Books Ltd, Registered Offices: Harmondsworth, Middlesex, England

First published in the United States of America by Viking and Puffin Books,
divisions of Penguin Putnam Books for Young Readers, 2000

3 5 7 9 10 8 6 4

LIBRARY OF CONGRESS CATALOGING-IN-PUBLICATION DATA
Ziefert, Harriet.
Presents for Santa / by Harriet Ziefert ; illustrated by Laura Rader.
p.   cm.
Summary: When Mrs. Mouse's many children tell her what they would like
to give Santa for Christmas instead of making a wish list for
themselves, they have a happy surprise.
ISBN 0-670-88390-5 (hardcover) — ISBN 0-14-038186-4 (paperback)
[1. Gifts—Fiction. 2. Christmas—Fiction. 3. Mice—Fiction. 4. Stories
in rhyme.] I. Rader, Laura, ill. II. Title.
PZ8.3.Z47 Pr 2000 [E]—dc21 99-050872

Puffin® and Easy-to-Read® are registered trademarks of Penguin Putnam Inc.

Printed in Hong Kong
Set in Bookman

Reading Level: 2.0

Presents
FOR
Santa

There once was a mother
who lived in a shoe.
She had so many children
she didn't know what to do . . .

for Christmas!

And then Mrs. Mouse
had a fine idea!
She'd do something different
for Christmas this year.

"When Santa gives presents
each year, we forget
that it's better to give
than always to get.

"So mousekins be nice
and don't make a fuss.
We'll give presents to Santa
from each one of us."

"I'll make a list.
I'll start with Mike.
What do you think
Santa would like?"

"Give him a bike!"
said Mike.

"Give him a pony!"
said Tony.

"Give him a panda!"
said Amanda.

"A dolly!" said Molly.

"A dolly!" said Polly.

"A teddy!"
said Freddy.

"A bat!"
said Matt.

"Get a pet!"
yelled Brett.

"Bye-bye,"
yelled Guy.

Mrs. Mouse took her list
and went to the store.

She shopped and shopped
till her feet were sore.

And guess what?

Tony got a pony.

Amanda got a panda.

Mike got a bike.

Molly got a dolly.

And Polly got a dolly.

Freddy got a teddy.

Matt got a bat.
Brett got a pet.

Guy got a tie.

And Mrs. Mouse got
hugs and kisses!

Then Mrs. Mouse said,
"Santa gave presents
to each one of you.

Don't you think Santa
needs something too?"

"Give him the cake
we all helped to bake!"

Merry Christmas to all!